MILES·LEWIS

WHIZ KID

MILES★LEWIS
WHIZ KID

by Kelly Starling Lyons
illustrated by Wayne Spencer

Penguin Workshop

PENGUIN WORKSHOP
An imprint of Penguin Random House LLC, New York

First published in the United States of America by Penguin Workshop,
an imprint of Penguin Random House LLC, New York, 2022

Visit us online at penguinrandomhouse.com.

Library of Congress Cataloging-in-Publication Data is available.

Manufactured in China

ISBN 9780593383520 (paperback)   10 9 8 7 6 5 4 3 2 1 TOPL
ISBN 9780593383537 (library binding)   10 9 8 7 6 5 4 3 2 1 TOPL

Design by Mary Claire Cruz

For my cousins,
my forever friends—KSL

Dedicated to my daughter, Ali,
and anyone else who wants to
make things; don't give up.
You're almost there—WS

CHAPTER ONE

Second Chance

You know it's science fair time when you see posters in the hallway showing kids with cool projects and people looking amazed. Erupting volcanoes. Soda bottle tornadoes. Bouncy eggs. As I checked out the pictures, a grin stretched across my face.

Soon I wasn't in the hallway of Brookside Elementary anymore.

I could see myself onstage saying thank you as someone handed me a golden medal. Usually, I didn't care about winning. But this was different. This was my do-over. I had to get it right.

Last year, I created a switch that controlled the flow of electricity and turned a light bulb on and off. I couldn't wait to set it up and let my friends try it out. Everybody said I was gonna get one of the spots to represent our school in the regional competition.

But as I walked around, I saw other projects that put mine to shame. I cheered for the winners, but walked away knowing I could

have done better. I promised myself
I would try harder this year. I was a
future scientist—time to show it.

"What's up, Miles?" my best
friend RJ said. I almost forgot he was
standing next to me. "You're staring
at that poster like it's a puzzle you
got to figure out. You coming
to class?"

"Yeah," I said. "Just thinking about the science fair. I'm going to be ready."

We entered Miss Taylor's sunny classroom and tucked our backpacks in our cubbies. My friend Jada was putting hers away, too. Jada and I were in science club together. I knew she would be as psyched as I was about the fair.

"You know what time it is?" I asked.

"Yep," she said, her braids and beads bouncing as she nodded. "Science fair. I want to do something really special. I'm getting started on my project as soon as I get home."

"I know you'll come up with something great."

"You will, too," Jada replied. "Got any ideas?"

"Not yet."

As we headed to our seats, I wondered what I might do. It had to be something interesting and creative that would wow the judges. What science question could I ask and investigate?

After the announcements, Miss Taylor hit the chime that called us to the orange-and-blue rug for our morning meeting.

Chirr.

"Who saw something different on

the walls when you came into school this morning?"

Lena's hand shot up.

"Science fair posters."

Smiles and cheers mixed with a few frowns and groans.

"I see we have different feelings about it," Miss Taylor said. "That's okay. Remember there's no perfect project. It's all about learning something new and having fun. You all can do that, right?"

My friends gave thumbs-up and nodded. Miss Taylor always knew what to say.

"Can we do anything we want, Miss Taylor?" Simone asked as the glitter on her shirt caught the light. "I want to make something that shows my shine."

"Sure, Simone," she said, smiling. "As long as you follow the guidelines. I'll put the details and schedule in everyone's take-home folder. Your projects are going to be fantastic. This year, you can work on your own or in teams."

Teams? I looked at Jada and saw her looking at me.

"Want to work together?" I mouthed.

She nodded.

Yes! There would be no stopping us.

As we got up, I saw Gabi talking to Jada. Then, I felt a nudge in my side.

"You know we gotta be a team," RJ said.

I felt a sinking feeling in my stomach. RJ didn't care about science. I tried to think quickly.

"I already promised Jada I'd work with her."

"That's okay. She can be on the team, too. We're going to the best."

I sighed and hoped I was worrying for nothing. Maybe RJ would get into it and come through on the work.

Jada came up to my seat.

"Gabi wants to work with us, too," she said. "Is that okay?"

I smiled weakly.

"Yeah."

Gabi was cool, but having a team of four was harder to manage than a team of two. What if we wanted to do different projects? What if we didn't get along? This team thing wasn't going to be as easy as I thought.

CHAPTER TWO

Diving In

On the bus ride home, RJ and I sat next to each other like always.

"We should get started on our science project soon," I said. "The first thing is coming up with the idea. What do you think we should do?"

"What's the rush?" RJ said. "We have time. I got a new racing video game. Want to play later?"

I sighed. He was losing focus
already. Was this how it was going
to be?

"Not today," I said as the bus
neared my stop. "All about science
tonight."

I hopped off and walked down the block to my house. Nana gave me a big hug when I came inside. She smelled like oregano, basil, and wildflowers. Her long silver locs were pulled up so they didn't get in her face. I could tell she had been in her garden.

"What's good, grandson?" she asked.

I remembered how my heart pounded when I saw the posters in the hallway this morning. It was a thrill like biking downhill with the wind in my face. I wished I felt that way now.

"It's time for the science fair," I said with dread, like I was talking about a test that was on the way.

"Miles DuBois, that doesn't sound like you. Why did you say it like that? What's going on?"

"Nothing. I just really want to make the regional competition this year. I should get started. I'll be down to set the table for dinner, okay, Nana?"

"Okay, Miles," she said, with one eyebrow raised. She studied me like she knew something else was up. "You know you can always talk to me."

Upstairs in my room, I dropped my *Minecraft* backpack on the floor and sank into my desk chair. My man, Black Panther, stared at me from the wall. Wakanda-level skills— that's what I needed right now. Then this fair would be in the bag.

Everybody thinks I'm a whiz at science. But right now, I didn't feel so smart. I wondered if working with the team was the way to go, or if I should have gone solo again. Oh well. I knew Jada would come through. I bet Gabi would, too. Now, RJ . . . I tried to think positive. He played around sometimes, but he could be serious when he wanted.

I flipped open my computer and started surfing through options.

What should our project focus on? We had to do something good. Biology, physics, chemistry? So many possibilities. I made a list to share with the rest of the team.

Before I knew it, the tangy smell of tomatoes reached my room. My stomach grumbled like it was saying *What are you waiting for?* How long had I been upstairs? I rushed down the steps and zoomed right into the kitchen.

"You've been working hard," Nana said. "Feeling better?"

I nodded.

"Come here," she said, scooping some meat sauce onto a spoon. "Try this for me."

Mmm-hmm. I could taste the spices and herbs from her garden. Just right.

"It's delicious, Nana," I said. "Doesn't need anything."

I saw that she had breading and fish out. I knew what she was making: fried catfish and spaghetti! Some people were surprised by that combo, but Nana said it was a soul food classic in her family. It's one of my favorites, too.

Momma and Daddy came in as I was setting the table.

"I see you, son," Daddy said, winking.

"Yes, sir," Momma agreed. "I like how you're helping."

I gave them hugs and finished up. They headed for the kitchen to see if Nana needed anything. When the food was ready, we said grace and dug in.

"I have a surprise for you,"
Momma said to me.

She let the suspense build for
a few moments to make it extra
dramatic.

"Come on, Momma," I said when I couldn't stand it any longer. She laughed.

"You know how you've been asking for a sleepover? Your cousin, Cam, is coming this weekend."

"Yes!"

Cam was an only child like me, so we claimed each other as brothers. We had lots of the same interests— bikes, video games, basketball, chess, science.

He would get how much the fair meant to me. Cam made it into the regional science competition last year. He didn't win, but I was proud of him for getting that far. Yeah, things were looking up with Cam on the way. Maybe he could tell me the key to success.

CHAPTER THREE

Family Affair

At school the next day, we had time to do research or talk in our groups. Some kids were still trying to figure out if they were going to do a project on their own or with friends. Others, like Jada's besties, Lena and Simone, who teamed up with Carson, jumped right in.

Jada, Gabi, RJ, and I headed for

the reading nook decked out with
rainbow pillows and beanbag chairs.
We settled in and got to work.

"I did some research yesterday,"
I said. "I looked at a lot of projects.
I really liked one that showed how
wind and solar power could be good
sources of energy."

"That's cool, Miles," Jada said. "A project I liked was making a maze to see if a plant could find its way to a light."

Gabi's eyes lit up.

"Creating a maze sounds fun," she said. "But I was thinking that we could do an experiment with markers, paint, or crayons—mixing art and science."

RJ frowned.

"Those sound all right," he said. "But don't we want something that will grab everyone's attention, something really exciting?"

"You have an idea?" I asked.

"No," he said. "But we need a project that will be a winner."

I rolled my eyes. RJ wanted to criticize, but didn't have anything to offer. I hoped he'd do some research by our next meeting.

Jada, Gabi, and I had such different ideas. And RJ still had to add his. How were we going to choose? Right when I was about to suggest keeping a running list and then voting, Miss Taylor said it was time to wrap up. We wouldn't have school again until Monday. I wished we could meet sooner. Then, I remembered Cam.

"Hey, why don't I ask my mom and dad if we can get together at my house this weekend?" I said. "My cousin is coming over. He made the regional competition last year. Maybe he could give us some tips."

Everyone was down for that. Now, I just had to check with my parents.

When Momma and Daddy got home that evening, I asked about having my friends over.

"Sure," Momma said. "I'll reach out to their folks and find out if they can drop by tomorrow afternoon."

I took the stairs two at a time, quickly reaching the top. Cam was coming. My team was going to meet at my house. Picking our project early would give us an edge. It was all working out.

I looked around my room and took out some of the things Cam and I loved to do together: my chess board and mini old-school video games like *Pac-Man* and *Donkey Kong*. I couldn't wait until he got here.

Nana knocked on my open door. "How are things going? Think of a project?"

"Getting there."

"I'm glad," she said. "I don't like my boy being all stressed out. I get to spend time with both of my brilliant grandsons tonight."

I saw lights through my blinds and raced to the window. It was Uncle Curt, Cam's dad, parking his blue Chevy in the driveway. I didn't want to be rude and leave my room with Nana still standing there. I eyed her as I shifted from foot to foot.

"Go on, Miles," she said, laughing. "I'm excited he's here, too."

When I got downstairs, Cam was already inside.

"Hey, Cuzzo," he said, and held out his hand for our special shake.

We gripped one way and then the other, pulled and snapped, and then brought it in for a hug.

"Good to see you, Miles," Uncle Curt said, smiling as he watched us. "Cam, your mom will pick you up

Sunday. Have a great time."

Ever since his parents separated, Cam spent a week at a time with each of them. He was still getting used to going back and forth.

I grabbed Cam's bag and carried it upstairs to my room.

"Looks like you got some new LEGO models," he said, looking at my displays. "This one for the Avengers is tight."

"Thanks," I said. "There's one we can work on together, too, if you want."

"This is going to be the best," Cam said.

"Boys, pizza's here," my dad yelled. "Come and get it."

He didn't have to tell us twice. The stairs rumbled as we rushed downstairs.

"Whoa," Daddy said. "You sure there are just two of you? Sounded like a stampede."

We laughed and plopped into our seats. My eyes popped as I checked out the spread. Three pizzas—bacon, ground beef, and veggie—and buffalo wings. Now, this was a party.

"Cam, what's new with you?" my mom said, serving herself a piece of what we call hamburger pizza, because of the ground beef. "It's good to have you over. It has been too long."

"My basketball team is going to the playoffs, and I'm working on a science fair project like Miles."

"You made it to regionals last year, didn't you?" Daddy said.

Cam nodded and finished chewing.

"It was amazing! Kids from all over were there. I've never seen so many cool projects. We did our best, but we didn't win."

"They better watch out this time," Daddy said. "Here comes Cameron Lewis, super scientist."

"I know that's right," Nana said, beaming at Cam.

It shouldn't have bothered me that he was getting some praise. But

I had to look down so no one would see me frowning. I was entering the fair, too. Cam and I were both good at science. Why couldn't they say something nice about me?

"Miles is having his team over tomorrow to nail down their project,"

Momma said. "Maybe you could help them out."

"Sure, Aunt Trina," Cam said.

That was my plan all along, but now the idea of Cam giving us tips bugged me. He was getting all the shine. Did I want him in the spotlight with my friends, too?

When Cam smiled at me, I felt lower than a slug. Here I was hating on Cam in my mind, and we were supposed to be brothers. What was wrong with me? The sleepover was sinking fast.

CHAPTER FOUR

Cool Cam

After dinner, Cam and I headed back to my room.

"Okay, what do we get into first, Cuz?" Cam asked.

"You pick."

He walked over to the handheld video games, kept *Donkey Kong*, and handed *Pac-Man* to me.

"How about we play on each and then we switch? High score gets to

choose what we do next."

"You're on," I said.

"You know you can't hang with me," he teased.

"What? We'll see about that."

Just like that, the weirdness between us was gone. It was back to old times. We talked haircuts—his new fade was fire. Then we worked on an Avengers LEGO set.

"Who do you think has the most tech skills: Iron Man or Shuri?" he asked.

"I got Shuri. How about you?"

"I don't know. Iron Man is crazy competition."

Then, I asked about the tough stuff—his new life.

"How are things going with Uncle Curt and Aunt Char?"

"It's different," Cam said. "Sometimes I miss the way things were when we all lived together. But I guess it's okay."

I'd overheard my mom talking to Nana one day. She said Aunt Char told her that the separation was an adjustment for everyone, but they were doing their best to make sure Cam knew they loved him and always had his back.

Saturday, we got up and went on a walk with Nana. Why did we do that? She left us in the dust.

"You boys are too young to be dragging," she said. "Work those legs. Come on and keep up."

Nana was no joke. We speed-walked two miles. By the time we got back, we needed a nap. We flopped onto the couch and watched some TV. Before we knew it, meeting time was almost here.

I got some bowls out for snacks. I knew Momma would say we had to eat something healthy, so I grabbed some popcorn and peaches. But it wouldn't hurt to have a little candy, too. I grabbed a handful of mini chocolate bars.

Jada arrived first.

"Cam, this is my friend Jada," I said when she came in. "She has a bigger rock collection than me. And you know how we were talking about

Shuri? Jada could be her little sister."

"Come on, Miles," she said, looking embarrassed. "I'm not all that."

"If Miles says you're a GOAT, I got to believe it," Cam said.

Jada grinned.

The doorbell rang again a few minutes later. It was Gabi and RJ. They showed up at the same time.

"This is Gabi," I said, introducing her to Cam. "She's one of the best artists in the school. And you've heard me talk about my best friend RJ," I said. "He's competitive and makes us all put in the work."

"Hey, Gabi," Cam said. "What's up, RJ?"

"What's up, Cool Cam," RJ said.

"What did you call me? I might have to use that."

RJ cheesed like he just got a present for his birthday.

"Miles, your cousin has swag. What happened to you?"

Everybody laughed. I knew it was a joke, but I didn't crack a smile. I tried to shake off the mood that was creeping in. I knew the best way to do that was to get down to work.

"We're going to be in here," I said, leading them to the dining room. We sat around the table.

"Why don't we start by sharing our ideas?"

Cam took it all in as we talked. Then, he shared his thoughts.

"What if you found a way to blend parts of what all of you like together? Think about it. Miles wants to do a project about energy. Jada talked

about a maze. Gabi wants to do something with art. How about you, RJ?"

"I had an idea, but after listening to you, I just thought of something else. How about a racetrack? Seeing how fast cars go on it can show energy. The track can twist and turn like a maze, and we can decorate it."

I was impressed. Not only was RJ taking the project seriously, he came up with something awesome.

"There you go," Cam said, holding out his hand. They gripped each other. My stomach dropped when they did a special handshake of their own.

"Great idea, RJ," I said, reminding myself to stop hating. "We could use marbles as the race cars and design the track they go on. We can mount it on a display board and put ramps at different angles to keep the marbles rolling to the bottom."

"I see where you're going," Jada said. "Maybe we could use different kinds of marbles like metal ones and glass ones."

"How about using other round things, too, like beads and gumballs?" Gabi said.

Jada's eyes sparkled.

"Love that," she said. "We can make a hypothesis of which one will have the fastest time on the track."

"Okay, team," Cam said.

Just like that, we had our project.

Cam was good. Before I could thank him, RJ jumped in.

"Cool Cam," RJ said. "You hooked us up. Let's have some snacks to celebrate."

I felt that nagging feeling bugging me again. I looked down and sighed while everyone chattered and dug into the treats.

"You okay, Miles?" Cam asked. "What's wrong?"

Something was bothering me. But how could I admit I was jealous of him? I faked a smile and pushed down my feelings.

"Nothing," I said. "I'm all right."

If only that were true.

CHAPTER FIVE

Getting Down to Business

We had our idea. Now, it was time to make it happen. Over the next couple of weeks, we talked about our project in class and met when we could.

At Jada's house, Gabi sketched out a backdrop for the marble race while Jada, RJ, and I started working on the track. I knew I had this. I brought different materials we could use like

foam tubing and craft sticks, but
every time I tried to get the marble
going, it fell off or got stuck. Nothing
seemed to work like I wanted.

We guessed the metal marble would be fastest on a track because it was the heaviest out of the small round objects. But how could we test our hypothesis if we didn't have a track that worked?

We wanted to create a tall track that had angled ramps and tunnels so that the objects would roll downhill fast but with control, flowing from one level to the next.

Gabi came over to help.

"Why don't we cut these paper towel rolls and see if they work?" she said.

RJ grabbed some scissors and sliced a roll in half.

"Like this?" he said.

"Yeah," Jada said. "Let's glue
the pieces on the display board
at different angles and see what
happens."

The marble raced down one ramp
and fell to the other, speeding down
that one, too, with no problem at all.

"Let's go!" RJ shouted, holding out
his fists for Jada and Gabi to bump.

"Wish Cool Cam was here to see this."

Cam? What, was I invisible? This was crazy. I was supposed to be in my element, but I couldn't even help with something simple. Some science whiz.

"What do you think, Miles?" Jada asked.

"Great job," I said, and meant it. But I wasn't used to feeling like this. After flashing a smile, I looked away and fidgeted. I wondered if science was my thing after all.

"Miles, you're slipping," RJ said, nudging me in the side. "I'm surprised you didn't come up with paper towel rolls for the ramps."

I knew he was playing, but it stung. I frowned.

"That's not cool, RJ," Jada said, studying my face. "We all pitched in."

But it already got to me.

"No, it's all right, Jada," I said. "You, RJ, and Gabi have everything together. You don't need me."

"Don't be like that," RJ said. "You know I was just playing."

"Whatever."

I sat down hard and looked away.

You know that silence that's louder than a shout? That's all there was. Just a deep quiet that made me wish I could hear their thoughts. But when I turned back, their eyes said it all. They just looked at me like they didn't know me and weren't sure what was going on.

Thankfully, Momma rang the doorbell and let me off the hook. I said goodbye to my friends and thank you to Ms. Keisha, Jada's mom, and hurried out the door. I could feel everyone's stares on my back as I left.

"You were in a rush," Momma

said when we got in the car. "Did everything go okay?"

"Yeah," I said, gazing out the window. "We made some good progress."

"You sure?"

"Uh-huh. We figured out what to use for the marble track, and the background Gabi designed is awesome."

"So why do you sound like you did when you lost your first basketball game?"

I knew Momma wouldn't let up until I told her.

"I just want to do my best," I said. "I didn't come through today the way I should've."

"You're always so hard on yourself," she said. "Your friends know you bring it. Maybe this was someone else's day to shine. And I have some news that might cheer you up: Uncle Curt has a work meeting, so Cam is having dinner with us tonight."

Usually, I'd be thrilled about extra Cam time. But I wasn't sure how to feel about him coming over. Momma said we had to run a few errands before heading home. We drove to the gas station and post office. I leaned my head back on the way to our house and closed my eyes.

"Miles," Momma called as she

parked the car. "We're here."

Cam was already there when we arrived.

"Hey, Cuzzo," he said when he spotted me. "RJ told me about your project. Sounds like you have a winner."

"Huh? He already told you? How?"

"Yeah, we exchanged numbers the last time we were at your house. He called me with the details."

Ugh. There was nothing wrong with RJ liking Cam. Any other day I'd be excited that my best friend and my best cousin were buddies. But today, that was just a little too much. I wasn't feeling it at all.

Cam reached out his hand for our

special shake. I pretended I didn't
see it.

"I have to go upstairs and do
some homework," I said. "You want
to come up?"

"No," Cam said. "I'm good. I'll see
you when you come down."

I wondered if Cam knew I snubbed
him. Thinking that he did made me

feel even worse. I dropped into my desk chair and stared at the ceiling. This science project was supposed to be my do-over, my chance to have another shot at repping the school. Why was everything falling apart?

When I came down, I was ready to start fresh. Then, I saw Cam in the kitchen with Nana. They were laughing, rolling out dough and cutting circles for tea cakes, another of my favorite treats. I always helped Nana make those cookies. But she didn't call me. Cam didn't let me know what they were doing, either. It was like I didn't matter at all.

"Miles, you're right on time," Nana

said. "Wash your hands and you can add the toppings."

She had the rainbow sprinkles and cinnamon sugar ready on the table.

"No, that's okay," I said. "You got your favorite to help you."

"Who do you think you're talking to, Miles?" Nana said. "You better watch that tone. You know I don't play favorites."

Cam looked like I'd hit him.

"I'm sorry," I said, and rushed to my room.

Daddy came in behind me.

"Miles, what was that about? You know better than to give Nana attitude. And you hurt Cam, too."

"I know," I said. "I didn't mean to. But first, it was my friends. Now, it's Nana. Everybody loves Cam. I know it's selfish, but what about me?"

"Miles, we all get a little jealous

sometimes," Daddy said. "But you
know Cam is dealing with a lot. That
one-on-one time with Nana meant a
lot to him."

"I know," I said, hanging my head.

"Hold your head up, son," he said.
"What's really wrong?"

"Seems like everyone is getting everything right and I just keep messing up," I said. "Science is supposed to be my thing. But nothing is going the way I want."

"Oh, so, everything goes right for scientists all the time? Is that how it works?"

Daddy didn't have to say anything else. It was like his question opened a door in my mind. I started seeing all the great scientists who had to keep trying before scoring success. Messing up was part of the process.

"Got it," I said.

He nodded and left me with my thoughts. Whew. Daddy was a Black history professor. Nothing he loved more than handing out assignments to teach something you didn't know. In a minute, he would have had me write a report.

I felt lighter, but I knew I had something to do. I found Cam outside sitting on the porch. I sat next to him. We said nothing for a little while and just listened to the chirping birds and roar of cars down the street.

"What did I do to you?" Cam said softly.

"Nothing, Cuz. You didn't do anything. I'm sorry for hating. I've just been feeling jealous because everyone is giving you all the attention. Nana. My friends. And I feel like everything I do is wrong.

Didn't mean to take it out on you."

"I get it," he said. "But I was looking forward to hanging out like we usually do. It's something I thought would never change."

He blew through his lips like a balloon losing air.

"It won't," I said. "Are we good, Cam?"

He didn't say anything for a minute. My stomach fell to my shoes. Then, he cracked a smile as his eyes twinkled.

"You know what's up. Cousins are forever."

He held out his hand for our special handshake. I took it this time and then brought it in for a hug.

"I haven't even asked how your science project is going," I said.

"You sure you want to hear?"

"Definitely."

As Cam rattled off what his team was doing, he lit up like a streetlamp at night.

"I don't care if I make it to the city competition or not," he said. "I can't wait to show Mom and Dad what we did."

Cam was right. Winning wasn't what it was about. Time to go back to having fun.

CHAPTER SIX

Show and Prove

When I got on the bus the next day, I saw that instead of saving a seat for me, RJ was sitting next to someone else. Wow. He really was mad at me.

"Hey, RJ," I said. "Hey, Carson."

Carson said hi. RJ nodded his head and kept talking like I interrupted their conversation.

I wondered if the rest of the team was feeling like he was.

Today was the day to talk to the class about our projects. My team already decided I would be the spokesperson. When I came into the room, I saw Jada. I smiled at her. She gave me a little wave. I tried to make eye contact with Gabi. She turned her head. This wasn't going to be easy.

During morning announcements, I went over what I was going to say in my head. I had a lot of making up to do.

"Okay, class," Miss Taylor said. "The science fair is next week. I'm proud of how hard you've been working. Let's hear more about your projects."

Simone's team went first. She, Lena, and Carson tested different ingredients to figure out which created the best slime.

"Wait until you see what we made," Simone said. "Some slime was too sticky. Some was hard. You get to try the one that worked. We used glitter glue in it. When you pull the slime, it really sparkles."

Kyla's team tested paper airplanes to find out which one flew the farthest. They made different types of planes. Then, they threw each one five times and got an average of how far each design got.

"At the fair, you get to guess which one flew farthest before seeing our results," Kyla said.

Then it was my turn.

"Making mistakes is part of science," I said as Miss Taylor nodded. "It's about working hard and learning something new as you try."

I looked at RJ, Jada, and Gabi.
"I have the best team," I said.
"When we had trouble making our
marble racetrack, they kept going
until they figured out a solution."

I filled the class in on Gabi, Jada, and RJ coming up with using paper towel rolls for the ramps and on Gabi's awesome backdrop.

"We all pitched in," RJ added.

Jada and Gabi smiled. Everyone said they couldn't wait to try the track.

At lunch, RJ and I sat together like we usually did.

"What you said about us was cool," he said.

"Sorry it took me so long," I said. "But I'm all in."

"I'm glad," he said, and then looked at me with a smirk. "I was getting tired of carrying the team."

"What?"

"Just kidding."

I laughed and elbowed him. RJ cracking jokes meant everything was back to normal.

On science fair day, my team held our heads high and strutted into the auditorium with our project, the Marvelous Marble Grand Prix. After setting it up, we walked around and checked out some of the other projects. There were balloon-powered cars, models of working lungs, projects that grew crystals in different liquids and showed if music helped with memory. Wow. We were blown away.

Kids lined up to try our racetrack.
The metal ball was the fastest
sometimes, but our data showed that
sometimes it was too close to call. We
had to keep testing, tweaking, and
learning. Just like real scientists.

When the announcements came on the next morning, the class hummed with excitement. Would one of us snag a spot to represent Brookside in the regional competition? After the pledge and weather, it was finally time for the science results. Friends crossed their fingers and leaned forward in their seats as Mrs. Keane, our assistant principal, got ready to reveal the winners. I made eye contact with Jada, RJ, and Gabi. No matter what, we'd made something special together.

"The winners are . . ."

When Mrs. Keane said the names, RJ and a few others groaned. Fifth graders took the top spots again.

"But we worked so hard," RJ said.

"That's okay," I said. "We did our best. We still have another year."

Jada smiled at me.

I knew she felt the same way. Part of being a scientist is continuing to try until you get it right.

When I got home, Nana was in the garden. I dropped my bag and helped her pull weeds.

"Do you think Cam could come over this weekend?" I asked. "Maybe him, RJ, and me could shoot hoops at the park."

"I'll talk to Curt," Nana said.

"Sounds like a plan. You know I'm always proud of you. But I'm especially proud today."

After finishing up, I washed my hands and headed to my room. The science fair didn't turn out like I thought it would, but I couldn't help but smile. My friends and I had done something special. Cam and I were back to being cousins and brothers.

Nothing was better than that.

Miles's Five Facts

My dad teaches Black history. He loves giving me assignments to learn more about important people and events. But this time, I did some digging on my own.

Here are some scientists I think are cool:

1. Dr. Kizzmekia S. Corbett was the lead scientist for the Coronavirus Vaccines Team at the US National Institutes of Health (NIH). She cried when she found out the Moderna vaccine she helped develop worked.

2. Some people call Dr. Percy Julian one of the most important chemists in US history. His discoveries helped create a treatment for

glaucoma, an eye disease, and arthritis, which causes joint problems.

3. Dr. Patricia Bath helped people see better. She invented a device and technique to remove cataracts, cloudiness on the lens of your eye.

4. Dr. Ernest Everett Just was a biologist who made a difference. He was a trailblazer who helped us better understand fertilization and the role of cells in development. He was also one of the founders of Omega Psi Phi Fraternity, Inc.

5. Annie Easley was a NASA computer and rocket scientist. She worked on Centaur technology to help boost rockets into space.

Acknowledgments

Every new book is an adventure. Thank you for coming with me on this one. I knew a science fair was something I wanted to explore in the series. Miles, like you, works hard and pushes himself to do his best. But sometimes he can forget that stumbling is part of learning.

No one is perfect, not even scientists. Making mistakes stretches the mind, helps develop new ideas, pushes us to keep trying. Like Miles and his friends, you're all whiz kids in different ways. Remember that when you're having a hard time figuring something out.

This series wouldn't be possible without: my brilliant editor Renee Kelly, the rock stars at Penguin Workshop, talented illustrator Wayne Spencer, my agent Caryn Wiseman, my kids Gabe and Josh, my beautiful family and friends, and all of you.